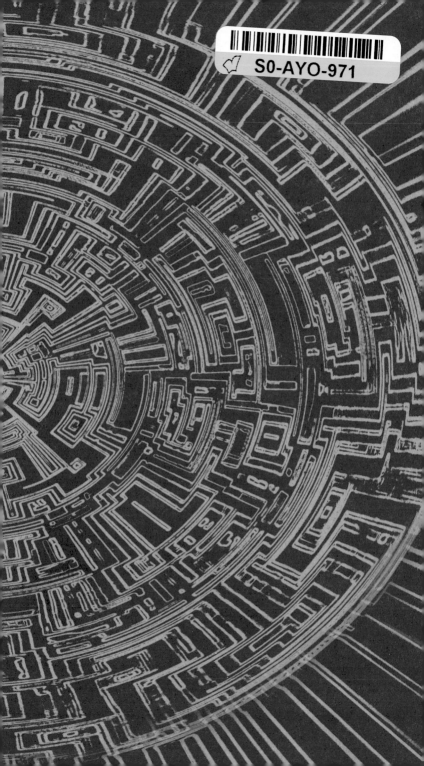

All About
Emily

All About Emily

Connie Willis

Illustrated by J. K. Potter

SUBTERRANEAN PRESS 2011

First Edition

ISBN
978-1-59606-452-2

Subterranean Press
PO Box 190106
Burton, MI 48519

www.subterraneanpress.com

"Fuck *The Red Shoes*. I wanted
to be a Rockette."

A Chorus Line

ALL RIGHT, SO YOU'RE probably wondering how I, Claire Havilland, three-time Tony winner, Broadway legend, and star of *Only Human*—ended up here, standing outside Radio City Music Hall in a freezing rain two days before Christmas, soaked to the skin and on the verge of pneumonia, accosting harmless passersby.

Well, it's all my wretched manager Torrance's fault. And Macy's. And the movie *All About Eve*'s.

You've never heard of *All About Eve*? Of course you haven't. Neither has anyone else. Except Emily.

It starred Anne Baxter and Bette Davis, and was the first movie Marilyn Monroe appeared in. She played Miss Caswell, a producer's girl-friend, but the movie's not about her. It's about an aging Broadway actress, Margo Channing, and the young aspiring actress, Eve Harrington, who insinuates herself into Margo's life and makes off with her starring role, her career, and very nearly, her husband.

All About Eve was made into a musical called *Applause* and then into a straight dramatic play which was then made into *another* musical (Broadway has never been terribly creative.) The second musical, which was called *Bumpy Night* and starred Kristin Stewart as Eve and me as Margo, only ran for three months, but it won me my second Tony and got me the lead in *Feathers*, which won me my third.

Macy's is a New York department store, in case you don't know that either. Except for Emily, no one today seems to know anything that happened longer than five minutes ago. Macy's sponsors a parade on Thanksgiving Day every year, featuring large balloons representing various cartoon characters, the stars of various Broadway shows waving frozenly from floats, and the Rockettes.

And my manager Torrance is a lying, sneaky, conniving snake. As you shall see.

The Wednesday night before Thanksgiving he knocked on my dressing-room door during intermission and said, "Do you have a minute, dear one? I've got *fabulous* news!"

I should have known right then he was up to something. Torrance only comes backstage when: one, he has bad news to deliver, or two, he wants something. And he never knocks.

"The show's closing," I said.

"*Closing!* Of course not. The house is sold out every night through Christmas. And it's no wonder! You get more dazzling with every performance!" He clutched his chest dramatically. "When you sang that Act I finale, the audience was eating out of your hand!"

"If you're still trying to talk me into having lunch with Nusbaum, the answer is no," I said, unzipping my garden party costume. "I am *not* doing the revival of *Chicago*."

"But you were the best Roxie Hart the show ever had—"

"That was twelve years ago," I said, shimmying out of it. "I have no intention of wearing a leotard at my age. I am too old—"

"Don't even *say* that word, dear one," he said, looking anxiously out into the hall and pulling the door behind him. "You don't know who might hear you."

"They won't have to hear me. One look at me in fishnet stockings, and the audience will be able to figure it out for themselves."

"Nonsense," he said, looking appraisingly at me. "Your legs aren't that bad."

Aren't that bad. "Dance ten, looks three?" I said wryly.

He stared blankly at me.

"It's a line from *A Chorus Line*, a show I was in which you apparently never bothered to see. It's a line which proves my point about the fishnet stockings. I am *not* doing *Chicago*."

"All Nusbaum's asking is that you meet him for lunch. What harm could that do? He didn't even say what role he wanted you for. It may not be Roxie at all. He may want you for the part of—"

"Who? The warden?" I said, scooping up my garden-party costume into a wad. "I told you I was too old for fishnet stockings, not old enough to be playing Mama Morton." I threw it at him. "Or Mama Rose. Or *I Remember Mama*."

"I only meant he might want you to play Velma," he said, fighting his way out of the yards of crinoline.

"No," I said. "Absolutely not. I need a role where I keep my clothes on. I hear Austerman's doing a musical version of *Desk Set*."

"*Desk Set*?" he asked. "What's it about?"

Apparently he never watched movies either. "Computers replacing office workers," I said. "It was a Julia Roberts-Richard Gere movie several years ago, and there are no fishnet stockings in it anywhere." I wriggled into my ball gown. "Was that all you wanted?"

I knew perfectly well it wasn't. Torrance has been my manager for over fifteen years, and one thing I've learned during that time was that he never gets around to what he really wants till Act Two of a conversation, apparently in the belief that he can soften me up by asking for some other thing first. Or for two other things, if what he wants is particularly unpleasant, though how it could be worse than doing *Chicago*, I didn't know.

"What did you come in here for, Torrance?" I asked. "There are only five minutes to curtain."

"I've got a little publicity thing I need you to do. Tomorrow's Thanksgiving, and the Macy's parade—"

"No, I am not riding on the *Only Human* float, or standing out in a freezing rain again saying, 'Look! Here comes the *Wall-E* balloon!'"

There was a distinct pause, and then Torrance said, "How did you know there's a *Wall-E* balloon in the parade? I thought you only read *Variety*."

"There was a picture of it on the home page of the *Times Online* yesterday."

"Did you click to the article?"

"No. Why? As you say, I never read the news. You didn't already tell them I'd do it, did you?" I said, my eyes narrowing.

"No, of course not. You don't have to go anywhere near the parade."

"Then why did you bring it up?"

"Because the parade's Grand Marshal is coming to the show Friday night, and I'd like you to let him come backstage after the performance to meet you."

"Who is it this year?" I asked. It was always a politician, or whatever talentless tween idol was going to be starring on Broadway next. "If it's any of Britney Spears' offspring, the answer is no."

"It's not," Torrance said. "It's Doctor Edwin Oakes."

"*Doctor?*"

"Of physics. Nobel Prize for his work on artificial neurotransmitters. He founded AIS."

"Why on earth is a physicist the Grand Marshal of the Macy's Day Parade?" I said. "Oh, wait, is he the robot scientist?"

There was another pause. "I thought you said you didn't read the article."

"I didn't. My driver Jorge told me about him."

"Where'd *he* hear about Dr. Oakes?"

"On the radio. He listens to it in the limo while he's waiting."

" Oh. What did Jorge tell you about him?"

"Just that he'd invented some new sort of robot that was supposed to replace ATMs and subway-ticket dispensers, and that I shouldn't believe it, they were going to steal all our jobs— Oh, my God, you're bringing some great, clanking Robbie the Robot backstage to meet me!"

"No, of course not. Don't be ridiculous. Would I do that?"

"Yes. And you didn't answer my question. *Is* this the same Doctor Oakes? The robot scientist?"

"Yes, only they're not robots, they're 'artificials.'"

"I don't care what they're called. I'm not granting a backstage interview to C3PO."

"You're dating yourself, dear one," he said. "C3PO was *eons* ago. The reason Dr. Oakes was asked to be the Grand Marshal is because this year's parade theme is robots, in honor of—"

"Don't tell me—*Forbidden Planet*, right? I should have known."

Forbidden Planet. The *second* worst show to ever have been on Broadway, but that hasn't stopped it from packing them in down the street at the Majestic, thanks to Robbie the Robot and a never-ending procession of pop idols (at this point it's Shiloh Jolie-Pitt and Justin Bieber, Jr.) in the starring roles. "And I suppose that's where this Dr. Oakes is tonight?"

"No, they didn't want to see *Forbidden Planet*—"

"They?" I said suspiciously.

"Dr. Oakes and his niece. They didn't want to meet Shiloh and Justin. They want to see *Only Human*. And to meet you."

I'll bet, I thought, waiting for Torrance to get to the real reason he'd come backstage to see me, because meeting a couple of fans couldn't be it. He dragged a ragtag assortment of people backstage every week. He wasn't still trying to talk me into doing the latest revival of *Cats*, was he? It was not only *the* worst musical ever produced on Broadway, but it required tights *and* whiskers.

"Dr. Oakes's niece is really eager to meet you," Torrance was saying. "She's a huge fan of yours. It will only take five minutes," he pleaded. "And it would really help with ticket sales."

"Why do the ticket sales need help? I thought you said we had full houses through Christmas."

"We do, but the weather's supposed to turn bad next week, and sales for after New Year's have been positively *limp*. Management's worried we won't last till January. And the word is Disney's scouting for a theater where they can put his new production of *Tangled*. If they get nervous about our closing—"

"I don't see how meeting them will help us get publicity. Physicists are hardly front-page news."

"I can guarantee it'll get us publicity. WNET's already said they'll be here to live-stream it. And Sirius. And when Emily said she wanted to meet you on *Good Morning, America* yesterday, ticket sales for this weekend went through the roof."

"I thought you said we were already sold out through Christmas."

"I said *Only Human* was playing to full houses."

Which meant half the tickets were going for half-price at the TKTS booth in Times Square and the back five rows of the balcony were roped off for "repairs."

"And you know what the management's like when they think they're going to love their investment. They'll jump at anything—"

"All right," I said. "I'll meet with Dr. Nobel Prize and his niece, if she *is* his niece. Which I seriously doubt."

"Why do you say that?" Torrance said sharply.

"Because all middle-aged men are alike. Her name wouldn't be Miss Caswell, would it?"

"Who?"

"The producer's girlfriend," I said. I pantomimed a pair of enormous breasts. "Ring a bell?" He looked blank. "Really, Torrance, you should at least *pretend* to have watched the plays I'm starring in."

"I do. I have. I just don't remember any Miss Caswell in *Only Human*."

"That's because she wasn't in *Only Human*. She was in *Bumpy Night*. Lindsay Lohan played her, remember?" and when he still looked blank, "Marilyn Monroe played her in the original movie. And please don't tell me you don't know who that is, or you'll make me feel even more ancient than I am."

"You're not ancient, dear one," he said, "and I wish you'd stop being so hard on yourself. You're a legend."

Which is a word even more deadly to one's career than "old" or "cellulite." And only slightly less career-ending than "First Lady of the Theater." I said, "Yes, well, this 'legend' just changed her mind. No backstage interview."

"Okay," he said. "I'll tell them no dice. But don't be surprised if they decide to go to *Forbidden Planet* instead. Their entire cast has agreed to a backstage interview, including Justin."

"All right, fine. I'll do it," I said. "If you get me out of the lunch with Nusbaum and talk to Austerman about *Desk Set*."

"I will. This interview will help on the *Desk Set* thing," he said, though I couldn't see how. "Star Meets Fans" is hardly home-page news. "You'll be glad you did this. You're going to like Emily."

There was only one thing to like about having been blackmailed into doing the interview: our discussion of it had taken up the entire intermission, and Torrance hadn't had time to ask me the thing he'd actually come backstage to ask.

I expected him to try again after the show, but he didn't. He left a message saying, "WABC will be there to film meeting. Wear something suitable for Broadway legend. *Sunset Boulevard*?" Which was either proof that he saw me much as I was beginning to see myself, as a fading (and deranged) star, or that he hadn't seen the musical *Sunset Boulevard* either.

I had the wardrobe mistress hunt me up the magenta hostess gown from *Mame* and a pair of *Evita* earrings, signed autographs for the fans waiting outside the stage door, turned my phone off, and went home to bed.

I kept my phone off through Thanksgiving Day so Torrance couldn't call me and insist I watch Dr. Oakes in the parade, but I didn't want to miss a possible call from Austerman about *Desk Set*, so Friday I turned my phone back on, assuming (incorrectly) that Torrance would call and make another attempt at broaching the subject of whatever it was he'd really come to my dressing room about.

Because it couldn't possibly be the scruffy-looking professor and his all-dressed-up niece who Torrance brought to my dressing room Friday night after the show. I could see why Torrance had rejected the idea of her being the producer's mistress. This petite, fresh-scrubbed teenager with her light brown hair and upturned nose and pink cheeks was nothing like Marilyn Monroe. She was nothing like the gangly, tattooed, tipped, and tattered girls who clustered outside *Forbidden Planet* every night either, waiting for Justin, Jr. to autograph their playbills.

This girl, who couldn't be more than five-foot-two, looked more like the character of Peggy in the first act of *42nd Street*, wide-eyed and giddy at being in New York City for the first time. Or a sixteen-year-old Julie Andrews. The sort of dewy-eyed innocent ingénue that every established actress hates on sight. And that the New York press can't wait to get its claws into.

But they were being oddly deferential. And they were all here. Not just *Good Morning, America*, but the other networks, the cable channels, the *Times*, the *Post-Daily News*, and at least a dozen bloggers and streamers.

"How'd you manage to pull this off?" I whispered to Torrance as they squeezed into my dressing room. Apart from the Tonys, *Spiderman III* accidents, and Hollywood stars, it's impossible to get the media to cover anything theatrical. "Lady Gaga's not replacing me in the role, is she?"

He ignored that. "Claire, dear one," he said, as if he were in a production of Noel Coward's *Private Lives*, "allow me to introduce Dr. Edward Oakes. And this," he said, presenting the niece to me with a flourish, "is Emily."

"Oh, Miss Havilland," she said eagerly. "It's so exciting to meet you. You were just wonderful."

Well, at least she hadn't said it was an honor to meet me, or called me a legend.

"I loved *Only Human*," she said. "It's the best play I've ever seen."

It would be probably the *only* play she'd ever seen, but Torrance had been right, this meeting was good publicity. The media were recording every word and obviously responding to Emily's smile, which even I had to admit was rather sweet.

"You sing and dance so beautifully, Miss Havilland," she said. "And you make the audience believe that what they're seeing is real—"

"You're Emily's favorite actress," Torrance cut in. "Isn't that right, Emily?"

"Oh, yes. I've seen all your plays—*Feathers* and *Play On!* and *The Drowsy Chaperone* and *Fender Strat* and *Anything Goes* and *Love, Etc.*"

"But I thought Torrance said this was your first time in New York," I said. And she was much too young to have seen *Play On!*. She'd have been five years old.

"It *is* my first time," she said earnestly. "I haven't seen the plays onstage, but I've seen all your filmed performances and the numbers you've done at the Tony Awards—'When They Kill Your Dream' and 'The Leading Lady's Lament.' And

I've watched your interviews on Youtube and read all your on-line interviews and listened to the soundtracks of *A Chorus Line* and *Tie Dye* and *In Between The Lines*."

"My, you are a fan!" I said. "Are you sure your name's Emily and not Eve?"

"Eve?" Dr. Oakes said sharply.

Torrance shot me a warning glance, and the reporters all looked up alertly from the Androids they were taking notes on. "Why would you think her name was Eve, Miss Havilland?" one of them asked.

"I was making a joke," I said, taken aback at all this reaction. And if I said it was a reference to Eve Harrington, none of them would have ever heard of her, and if I said she was a character in *Bumpy Night*, none of them would have heard of that either. "I..."

"She called me Eve because I was doing what Eve Harrington did," Emily said. "That's who you meant, isn't it, Miss Havilland? The character in the musical *Bumpy Night*?"

"I...y-yes," I stammered, trying to recover from the shock that she'd recognized the allusion. The younger generation's knowledge usually doesn't extend farther back than *High School Musical: The Musical*.

"When Eve meets the actress Margo Channing," Emily was cheerfully telling the reporters, "she gushes to her about what a wonderful actress she is."

"*Bumpy Night*?" one of the reporters said, looking as lost as Torrance usually does.

"Yes," Emily said. "The musical was based on the movie *All About Eve*, which starred Bette Davis and Anne Baxter."

"And Marilyn Monroe," I said.

"Right," Emily said, dimpling. "As Miss Caswell, the producer's girlfriend. It was her screen debut."

I was beginning to like this girl, in spite of her perfect skin and perfect hair and the way she could hold an audience. The media were hanging on her every word. Although that might be because they were as astonished as I was at a teenager's knowledge of the movies.

"—Marilyn Monroe was in *Gentlemen Prefer Blondes* and *How to Marry a Millionaire*," she said, "which Lauren Bacall was in, too. She starred in the first musical they made of *All About Eve*, *Applause*. It wasn't nearly as good as *Bumpy Night*, or as faithful to the movie."

And since she knew so much about movies, maybe this was a good time to put in a pitch for my doing Austerman's play. "Have you ever seen *Desk Set*, Emily?" I asked her.

"Which one? The Julia Roberts-Richard Gere remake or the original with Katherine Hepburn and Spencer Tracy?"

Good God. "The original."

"Yes, I've seen it. I *love* that movie."

"So do I," I said. "Did you know they're thinking of making a musical of it?"

"Oh, you'd be wonderful in the Katherine Hepburn part!"

I definitely liked this girl.

"What about *Cats*?" Torrance asked.

I glared at him, but he ignored me.

"Have you ever seen the musical *Cats*?" he persisted.

"Yes," she said and wrinkled her nose in distaste. "I didn't like it. There's no plot at all, and 'Memories' is a terrible song. *Cats* isn't nearly as good as *Only Human*."

"You see, Torrance?" I said and turned my widest smile on Emily. "I'm so glad you came to the show tonight."

"So am I," she said. "I'm sorry I sounded like Eve Harrington before. I wouldn't want to be her. She wasn't a nice person," she explained to the reporters. "She tried to steal Margo's part in the play from her."

"You're right, she wasn't very nice," I said. "But I suppose one can't blame her for wanting to be an actress. After all, acting's the most rewarding profession in the world. What about you, Emily? Do you want to be an actress?"

It should have been a perfectly safe question. Every teenaged girl who's ever come backstage to meet me has been seriously stage-struck, especially after seeing their first Broadway musical, and Emily *had* to be, given her obsessive interest in the movies and my plays.

But she didn't breathe, "Oh, yes," like every other girl I'd asked. She said, "No, I don't."

You're lying, I thought.

"I could never do what you do, Miss Havilland," Emily went on in that matter-of-fact voice.

"Then what *do* you want to do? Paint? Write?"

She glanced uncertainly at her uncle and then back at me.

"Or does your uncle want you to be a neuro-physicist like him?" I asked.

"Oh, no, I couldn't do that either. Any of those things."

"Of course you could, an intelligent girl like you. You can do anything you want to do."

"But I—" Emily glanced at her uncle again, as if for guidance.

"Come, you must want to be something," I said. "An astronaut. A ballerina. A real boy."

"Claire, dear one, stop badgering the poor child," Torrance said with an artificial-sounding laugh. "She's in New York for the very first time. It's scarcely the time for career counseling."

"You're right, I'm sorry, Emily, " I said. "How are you liking New York?"

"Oh, it's wonderful!" she said.

The eagerness was back in her voice, and Dr. Oakes had relaxed. Did she want to go on the stage and her uncle didn't approve? Or was something else going on? "How are you liking New York?" was hardly riveting stuff, but there wasn't a peep out of the media. They were watching us raptly, as if they expected something to happen at any second.

I should have read the article in the Times, I thought, and asked Emily if she'd been to the Empire State Building yet.

"No," she said, "we do that tomorrow morning after we do *NBC Weekend*, and then at ten

I'm going ice-skating at Rockefeller Center. It would be wonderful if you could come, too."

"At ten in the morning?" I said, horrified. "I'm not even up by then," and the reporters laughed. "Thank you for asking me, though. What are you doing tomorrow night?" I asked and then realized she was likely to say, "We're seeing *Forbidden Planet*." But I needn't have worried.

"We're going to see the Christmas show at Radio City Music Hall," she said.

"Oh, good. You'll love the Rockettes. Or have you seen them already? They were in the parade, weren't they?"

"No," Emily said. "What are—?"

"They don't ride in the parade," Torrance said, cutting in. "They dance outside Macy's on Thirty-fourth Street. What else are you and your uncle doing tomorrow, Emily?"

"We're going to Times Square, and then Macy's and Bloomingdale's to see the Christmas windows, and then FAO Schwarz—"

"Good God," I said. "All in one day? It sounds exhausting!"

"But I don't—" Emily began.

This time it was Dr. Oakes who cut in. "She's too excited at being here to be tired," he said.

"There's so much to see and do. Emily's really looking forward to seeing the Rockettes, aren't you?" He nodded at her, as if giving her a cue, and the reporters leaned forward expectantly. But they weren't looking at her, they were looking at me.

And suddenly it all clicked into place—their wanting to avoid the subject of her being tired, and Torrance's wanting to know what I'd read about the parade and Emily's encyclopedic knowledge of plays and the *Wall-E* balloon.

The parade's robot theme wasn't in honor of *Forbidden Planet*. It was in honor of Dr. Oakes and his "artificials," one of which was standing right in front of me. And those cheeks were produced by sensors, that wide-eyed look and dimpled smile were programmed in.

Torrance, the little rat, had set me up. He'd *counted* on the fact that I only read *Variety* and wouldn't know who Emily was.

And no wonder the media was all here. They were waiting with bated breath for the moment when I realized what was going on. It would make a great Youtube video—my shocked disbelief, Dr. Oakes's self-satisfied smirk, Torrance's laughter.

And if I hadn't tumbled to it, and she'd managed to fool me all the way to the end of the

interview with me none the wiser, so much the better. It would be evidence of what Dr. Oakes was obviously here to prove—that his artificials were indistinguishable from humans.

Emily really is *Eve Harrington*, I thought. *Innocent and sweet and vulnerable-looking. And not at all what she appears to be.*

But if I said that, if I suddenly pointed an accusing finger at her and shouted, "Impostor!" it would blow the image Dr. Oakes and AIS were trying to promote and make Torrance furious. And, from what I'd seen so far, Emily might be capable of bursting into authentic-looking tears, and I'd end up looking like a bully, just like Margo Channing had at the party at the end of Act One of *Bumpy Night*, and there would go any chance I had of getting the lead in *Desk Set*.

But if I went on pretending I hadn't caught on and continued playing the part Torrance had cast me in in this little one-act farce, I'd look like a prize fool. I could see the headline crawl on the *Times* building in *Times Square* now: "Bumpy Night For Broadway Legend." And "Robot Fools First Lady of the Theater." Not exactly the sort of publicity that gets an actress considered for a Tony.

Plus, the entire point of *Desk Set* was that humans are smarter than technology. *What would Katherine Hepburn do in this situation?* I wondered. *Or Margo Channing?*

"You'll love the Christmas show," Torrance was saying. "Especially the nativity scene. They have real donkeys and sheep. And camels."

"I'm sure it will be wonderful," Emily said, smiling winsomely over at me, "but I don't see how it can be any better than *Only Human*."

Only human. Of course. That was why they'd wanted to see the play and come backstage to trick me. *"Fasten your seat belts,"* I said silently. *"It's going to be a bumpy night."*

"And you'll love Radio City Music Hall itself," Torrance said. "It's this beautiful Art Deco building."

Dr. Oakes nodded. "They've offered to give us a tour before the show, haven't they, Emily?"

This was my cue. "Emily," I repeated musingly. "That's such a pretty name. You never hear it anymore. Were you named after someone?"

The reporters looked up as one from their corders and Androids and Dr. Oakes tensed visibly. Which meant I was right.

"Yes," Emily said. "I was named after Emily Webb from—"

"*Our Town*," I said, thinking, *Of course*. It was perfect. Except for Little Eva in *Uncle Tom's Cabin*, Emily Webb was the most sickeningly-sweet ingénue to ever grace the American stage, tripping girlishly around in a white dress with a big bow in her hair and prattling about how much she loves sunflowers and birthdays and "sleeping and waking up," and then dying tragically at the beginning of Act Three.

"It was her mother's favorite play," Dr. Oakes said. "And Emily was her favorite character."

"Oh," I said, and added casually, "I hadn't realized she was named after someone. I'd just assumed it was an acronym."

"An acronym?" Dr. Oakes said sharply.

"Yes, you know, MLE. For 'Manufactured Lifelike Entity' or something."

There was a dead silence, like the one that follows the revelation that I'm Hope's daughter in the third act of *Only Human*, and the reporters began to thumb their Androids furiously.

I ignored them. "And then I thought it might be your model number," I said to Emily. "Was your face modeled on Martha Scott's? She—"

"Played Emily Webb in the original production, which starred Frank Craven as the Stage Manager," Emily said. "No, actually, it was modeled on JoAnn Sayers, who played Eileen in—"

"The original Broadway production of *My Sister Eileen*," I said.

"Yes," she said happily. "I wanted to be named Eileen, but Uncle—I mean, Dr. Oakes—was worried that the name might suggest the wrong things. Eileen was much sexier than Emily Webb."

And she'd caused an uproar everywhere she went, ending up with half of New York and the entire Brazilian Navy following her in a wild conga line, something I was sure Dr. Oakes didn't want to have happen with his artificial.

"Women sometimes find sexiness in other women intimidating," Emily said. "I'm designed to be non-threatening."

"So of course the name Eve was out, too?"

"Yes," she said earnestly. "But we couldn't have used it anyway. It tested badly among religious people. And there was the *Wall-E* problem. Dr. Oakes didn't want a name that made people immediately think of robots."

"So I suppose the Terminator was out, as well," I said dryly. "And HAL."

The media couldn't restrain themselves any longer. "When did you realize Emily was an artificial?" the *Times* reporter asked.

"From the moment I saw her, of course. After all, acting is my specialty. I knew at once she wasn't the real thing."

"What tipped you off exactly?" the Youtube reporter said.

"Everything," I lied. "Her inflection, her facial expressions, her timing—"

Emily looked stricken.

"But the flaws were all *very* minor," I said reassuringly. "Only someone—"

I'd started to say "Only someone who's been on the stage as long as I have," but caught myself in time. "Only a pro could have spotted it," I said instead. "Professional actors can spot someone acting when the audience can't."

And that had better be true, or they'd realize I was lying through my teeth. "You're very, very good, Emily," I said and smiled at her.

She still looked upset, and even though I knew it wasn't real, that there was no actual emotion behind her troubled expression, her bitten lip, I said, "I'm not even certain *I* would have spotted it except that you were so much more knowledgeable about the theater than the young women who usually come backstage. Most of them think *A Little Night Music* is a song from *Twilight: The Musical*."

All but two of the reporters laughed. They— and Torrance—looked blank.

"You're simply too intelligent for your own good, darling," I said, smiling at her. "You should take a lesson from Carol Channing when she played—"

"Lorelei Lee in *Gentlemen Prefer Blondes*," she said, and then clapped her hand to her mouth.

The reporters laughed.

"But what really tipped me off," I said, squeezing her lifelike-feeling shoulder affectionately, "was that you were the only person your age I've ever met who wasn't stage-struck."

"Oh, dear." Emily looked over at Dr. Oakes. "I *knew* I should have said I wanted to be an actress." She turned back to me. "But I was afraid that might give the impression that I wanted your job, and of course I don't. Artificials don't want to take *anyone*'s job away from them."

"Our artificials are designed solely to help humans," Dr. Oakes said, "and to do only tasks that make humans' jobs easier and more pleasant," and this was obviously the company spiel. "They're here to bring an end to those machines everyone hates—the self-service gas pump, the grocery store checkout machine, electronic devices no one can figure out how to program. Wouldn't you rather have a nice young man fixing the bug in your computer than a repair program? Or have a friendly, intelligent operator connect you to the person you need to talk to instead of trying to choose from a dozen options, none of which apply to your situation? Or—" he nodded at me, "tell you who starred in the original production of a musical rather than having to waste time looking it up on Google?"

"And you can do all that?" I asked Emily. "Pump gas and fix computers and spit out twenties?"

"Oh, no," she said, her eyes wide. "I'm not programmed to do any of those things. I was designed to introduce artificials to the public."

And to convince them they weren't a threat, to stand there and look young and decorative. Just like Miss Caswell.

"Emily's merely a prototype," Dr. Oakes said. "The actual artificials will be programmed to do a variety of different jobs. They'll be your maid, your tech support, your personal assistant."

"Just like Eve Harrington," I said.

"What?" Dr. Oakes said, frowning.

"Margo Channing hired Eve Harrington as her personal assistant," Emily explained, "and then she stole Margo's career."

"But that can't happen with artificials," Dr. Oakes said. "They're programmed to assist humans, not supplant them." He beamed at me. "You won't ever have to worry about an Eve Harrington again."

"Dr. Oakes, you said they're forbidden to take our jobs," one of the reporters called out, "but if they're as intelligent as we've just seen Emily is, how do we know they won't figure out a way to get around those rules?"

"Because it's not a question of rules," Dr. Oakes said. "It's a question of programming. A human could 'want' someone else's job. An artificial can't. 'Wanting' is not in their programming."

"But when I asked Emily about her name," I reminded him, "she said she originally wanted to be called Eileen."

"She was speaking metaphorically," Dr. Oakes said. "She didn't 'want' the name in the human sense. She was expressing the fact that she'd made a choice among options and then altered that choice based on additional information. She was simply using the word 'want' as a shortcut for the process."

And to persuade us she thinks just like we do, I thought. In other words, she was acting. "And what about when she said she loved the play?" I asked him.

"I *did* love it," Emily said, and it might all be programming and sophisticated sensors, but she looked genuinely distressed. "Our preferences are just like humans."

"Then what's to keep them from 'preferring' they had our jobs?" the same reporter asked.

"Yeah," another one chimed in. "Wouldn't it be safer to program them not to have preferences at all?"

"That's not possible," Emily said. "Simulating human behavior requires higher-level thinking, and higher-level thinking requires choosing between options—"

"And often those options are equally valid," Dr. Oakes said, "the choice of which word or facial expression to use, of which information to give or withhold—"

Like the fact that you're an artificial, I thought, wondering if Dr. Oakes would include in his lecture the fact that higher-level thinking involved the ability to lie.

"Or the option of which action to take," he was saying. "Without the ability to choose one thing over another, action, speech—even thought—would be impossible."

"But then what keeps them from 'choosing' to take over?" a third reporter asked.

"They've been programmed to take into consideration the skills and attributes humans have which make them better qualified for the vast majority of jobs. But the qualities which cause humans to *desire* jobs and careers are not programmed in—initiative, drive, and the need to stand out individually."

"Which means your job's safe, Claire," Torrance said.

"Exactly," Dr. Oakes said without irony. "In addition, since artificials' preferences are not emotion-based, they lack the lust for power, sex, and money, the other factors driving job-motivation. *And*, as a final safeguard, we've programmed in the impulse to please humans. Isn't that right, Emily?"

"Yes," she said. "I wouldn't want to steal anybody's job. Especially yours, Miss Havilland."

Which is exactly what Eve Harrington said, I thought.

But this was supposed to be a photo-op, not a confrontation, and it was clear the reporters—and Torrance—had bought her act hook, line, and sinker, and that if I said anything, I'd come off just like Margo Channing at the party—as a complete bitch.

So I smiled and posed for photos with Emily and when she asked me if I'd go with them to the Radio City Music Hall Christmas Show ("I'm sure the Mayor can get us an extra ticket") I didn't say, "Over my dead body."

I said regretfully, "I have a show to do, remember?" And to make Torrance happy, "All of you out there watching, come see *Only Human* at the Nathan Lane Theater on West Forty-fourth Street. Eight o'clock."

★

"You were absolutely marvelous!" Torrance said after everyone had gone. "Your best performance ever! We'll be sold out through Easter. I don't suppose you'd be willing to reconsider doing the ice-skating-at-Rockefeller-Center thing? It would make a great photo-op. All you'd have to do is put on a cute little skating skirt and spend half an hour gliding around—"

"No skating skirts," I said, stripping off my earrings. "No tights. No—"

"No leotards. Sorry, I forgot. Maybe we can get her back here for a tour of the theater. If we can, we'll be sold out all the way through summer. Or you could invite her to your apartment for luncheon tomorrow."

"No luncheon," I said, wiping off my makeup. "No tours. And no robots."

"Artificials," he corrected automatically, and then frowned. "I thought you liked Emily."

"That's called acting, darling."

"But why don't you like her?"

"Because she's dangerous."

"Dangerous? That sweet little thing?"

"Exactly. That sweet little innocent, adorable, utterly harmless Trojan horse."

"But you heard Dr. Oakes. His artificials are programmed to help people, not steal their jobs."

"And they said movies wouldn't kill vaudeville, the synthesizer wouldn't replace the theater orchestra, and CGI sets wouldn't replace the stage crew."

"But you heard him, they've put in safeguards to prevent that. And even if they hadn't, Emily couldn't replace you. She can't act."

"Of course she can act. What do you think she was doing in here for the last hour? Mimicking emotions one doesn't have—I believe that's the definition of acting."

"I can't believe you're worried about this. No one could replace you, Claire. You're one of a kind. You're a—"

"Don't you dare say 'legend.'"

"I was going to say 'a star.' Besides, you heard Emily. She doesn't want to be an actress."

"I heard her, but that doesn't mean she won't be waiting outside that stage door when I leave, asking if she can be my assistant. And the next thing you know, I'll be stuck in the middle of Vermont, out of gas and out of a job."

"Vermont?" Torrance said blankly. "Why are you going to Vermont? You're not thinking of doing summer stock this year, are you?"

Which made me wonder if I should hire her as my personal assistant after all, just to have *someone* around who'd actually seen *Bumpy Night*. And knew what "Dance ten, looks three" meant.

But she wasn't in the crowd of autograph seekers—a crowd considerably smaller than that outside the Majestic, where *Forbidden Planet* was playing, I couldn't help notice. Nor was she waiting by the limo, nor at my apartment, already making herself at home, like Eve had done in Scene Three.

And she wasn't outside my door when I got up the next morning. The *Post-Daily News* was, no doubt left there by Torrance, with a very nice write-up—a photo and two entire columns about the backstage visit, which I was happy to see did not refer to me as a legend, and half an hour later

Torrance called to tell me *Only Human* was sold out through February. "And it's all thanks to you, darling."

"Flattery will get you nowhere," I said. "I'm still not going ice-skating."

"Neither is Emily," he said. "It's pouring rain outside."

Good, I thought. Emily would have to go convince the public she wasn't a threat to them at the Chrysler Building or MOMA or something. *Or if she's such a huge fan of mine, maybe she'll come see* Only Human *again*. But she wasn't in the audience at the matinee.

I was relieved. In spite of Dr. Oakes's assurances that AIS's artificials weren't here to steal our jobs and Emily's earnest protestations that she didn't want to be an actress, the parallels to *All About Eve* were a bit too close for comfort. I mean, who were we kidding? If artificials weren't a threat, Dr. Oakes and AIS wouldn't be expending so much time and effort convincing us they weren't.

So I wasn't at all unhappy when the rain turned into a sleety downpour just before the evening performance, even though it meant there were cancellations and the audience that did come out smelled like wet wool. They coughed and sneezed their way through both acts and dropped their umbrellas noisily on every important line, but at least Emily wouldn't be waiting for me outside the stage door afterward like Eve Harrington in Scene Two of *Bumpy Night*.

In fact, no one was at the stage door or out front, though the sleet apparently hadn't stopped the *Forbidden Planet* fans down the street. A huge crowd of them huddled under umbrellas, clutching their sodden *Playbills*, waiting for Shiloh and Justin, Jr. So much for Torrance's saying my meeting with Emily would bring in the younger demographic.

My driver Jorge splashed toward me with an open umbrella. I ducked gratefully under its shelter and let him shepherd me toward the waiting limo and into the back seat.

I sat down and shook out the tails of my coat while he went around to the driver's side, and then I bent to see how much damage had been done to my shoes.

A girl was banging on my window with the flat of her hand. I could see the hand but not who it was through the fogged-up window. But whoever it was knew my name. "Miss Havilland!"

she called, her voice muffled by the closed window and the traffic going by. "Wait!"

Shiloh and Justin aren't the only ones with fans who are willing to freeze to death to get an autograph, I thought and fumbled with the buttons in the door, attempting to roll down the window. "Which button is it?" I asked Jorge as he eased his bulk into the driver's seat.

"The one on the left," he said, slamming his door and starting the car. "If you want, I can drive off."

"And leave a fan?" I said. "Heaven forbid," even though with the week I'd had it would probably only turn out to be a *Forbidden Planet* fan who'd gotten tired of waiting and decided to get my autograph instead of Justin's so she could get in out of the sleety rain. "Signing autographs is a Broadway legend's duty," I said and pushed the button.

"Oh, *thank* you, Miss Havilland," the girl said, clutching the top of the window as it began to roll down. "I was afraid you were going to drive away."

It was Emily, looking like a drowned rat, her light-brown hair plastered to her forehead and cheeks, rain dripping off her eyelashes and nose.

"What are you doing here?" I demanded, though it was obvious. This was exactly like the scene in *Bumpy Night* when Eve told Margo Channing she hadn't eaten for days because she'd spent all her money on tickets to Margo's play.

"I have to talk to you," she said urgently, and I had to admire Dr. Oakes's engineering genius. Emily's cheeks and nose were the vivid red of freezing cold, her lips looked pale under her demure pink lipstick, and the knuckles of her hands, clutching the rolled-down window, were white.

She's not really cold, I told myself. *That's all done with sensors. They're programmed responses.* But it was difficult not to feel sorry for her standing there, the illusion was so perfect.

And it had obviously convinced Jorge. He leaned over the back seat to ask, "Shouldn't you ask her to get in the car?"

No, I thought. *If I do, she'll tell me some sob story, and the next thing you know I'll be hiring her on as my understudy. And I have no intention of being the next Margo Channing, even if she does look pathetic.*

I didn't say that. I said, "Where's Dr. Oakes? I thought you two were supposed to go see the Christmas show at Radio City Music Hall tonight."

"We were...we...I did," she stammered. "But something happened—"

"To Dr. Oakes?" I said and had a sudden image of her killing him like Frankenstein's monster and rampaging off into the night.

"No," she said. "He doesn't know I'm gone. I sneaked away so I could talk to you about what happened. Something...I...something happened to me while I was watching the show."

Of course. "And you decided you want to be an actress after all," I said dryly, or rather, with as much dryness as it was possible to muster with gusts of icy rain blowing on me.

Her eyes widened in a perfect imitation of astonishment. "No. Please, Miss Havilland," she pleaded. "I *have* to talk to you."

"You can't just let her stand out there like that," Jorge said reproachfully. "She'll catch pneumonia."

No, she won't, I thought, but he was right. I couldn't just let her stand out there. The water might short out her electronics or rust her gears or something. And if anyone happened to see her standing there, begging to be let in, I'd look like a monster.

And even if I told them she was a robot, they'd never believe it, seeing her standing there with her red nose and blue lips. And now her teeth were chattering, for God's sake. "Get in the car," I said.

Jorge hurried around to open the door for Emily, and she scrambled in, getting water everywhere. "Thank you *so* much, Miss Havilland," she said, grabbing my hand, and her sensors were even better than I'd thought they were. Her hands felt exactly as icy as a fan's would have standing out in that sleety rain.

"Turn on the heat," I ordered Jorge. "Emily, where were you when you sneaked away from Dr. Oakes? At Radio City Music Hall?"

"Yes. I told him I needed to go to the ladies' room off the Grand Lounge."

The ladies' room? Just how authentic was she?

"To see the murals," she said. "They were done by Witold Gordon, and they show the history of cosmetics through the ages—Cleopatra and the Greeks and Marie Antoinette and—"

"And something happened to you in the ladies' room?"

"No," she said, frowning. "I told him I was going to the ladies' room so I could sneak out the side door.

Definitely able to lie, I thought "How long ago was this?" I asked her.

"Eighteen minutes. I ran all the way."

Less than twenty minutes, which hopefully meant Dr. Oakes hadn't panicked yet and filed a "Missing Robot" report. "Jorge, give me your phone," I said.

He did.

"Emily, what's Dr. Oakes's cell phone number?"

"Oh, don't send me back!"

"I won't," I promised. "Tell me his number."

She did.

"This is Claire Havilland," I told him when he answered. "I called to tell you not to worry— Emily's with me. I'm giving her a tour of the theater and then we're going out for some authentic New York cheesecake."

"She can't eat cheesecake. She's an artifi—"

"Yes, I know, but *I* can eat it, and I thought she'd enjoy seeing a genuine theatre-district deli. I'll bring her home afterwards. Are you at your hotel?"

He wasn't, he was still at Radio City Music Hall. "The staff and I have been looking for her everywhere. I was about to call the police. Why didn't she tell me you were giving her a tour?"

"It was a simple case of miscommunication," I said to distract him. "She thought I'd told you, and I thought you were there when we discussed it," I said, hoping he wouldn't remember we hadn't had any opportunity to talk alone, that he'd been there the entire time. "I am *so* sorry about the mixup, Dr. Oakes."

"She still should have told me she was leaving," he said. "She should have known I'd be worried."

"How could she?" I said. "As you said, she doesn't have human emotions."

"But I specifically programmed her to—"

He wasn't going to let go of it. "You sound hoarse," I said. "Are you catching a cold?"

"I probably am. I got drenched standing out front waiting for her. If I catch pneumonia because of this—"

"You poor thing," I said, summoning every bit of acting ability I'd acquired over the last twenty-five years in order to sound sympathetic. "Go straight home and get into bed. And have room service send you up a hot toddy. I'll take care of Emily and see she gets home safely," and after a few more disgruntled-parent sounds, he hung up.

"There," I said. "That's taken care of—"

"Are we really going to a deli?" Emily asked unhappily.

"No, not unless you want to. I just told him that to keep him from coming here to the theater. Where would you like to go? Back into the theater? I think Benny's still here. He could let us in."

"Could we just stay here in the car?"

"Certainly," I said and told Jorge to pull in closer to the curb.

He did and then got a plaid blanket out of the trunk and put it over Emily's knees. "Oh, but I don't—" she began.

I shook my head at her.

She nodded and let him cover her knees with the blanket and drape his jacket around her shoulders. "Thank you," she said, smiling enchantingly up at him.

"Would you like something hot to drink?" he asked her as if he'd forgotten I was even in the car. "Coffee or—?"

"Oh, no," she said. "I'm afraid I can't—"

"She'll have cocoa," I interrupted, thinking how much I would give to be able to look as young and helplessly appealing as she did, "and bring me a coffee with a shot of rum in it. Not that mud they make at Dark Brew," I added. "Go to Finelli's." Which was six blocks away.

He trotted off obediently. "Good," I said. "Now we can talk. Tell me what's happened. You went to see the Christmas show at Radio City Music Hall…"

"Yes, and it's beautiful. It's *huge*, with gold curtains and chandeliers and statues and this enormous stage—"

"I know. I've been there. You said something happened?"

"Yes, the show started and there was all this singing and dancing, and then the Rockettes came out. They're this group of forty dancers—there were originally sixteen of them, called the Roxyettes, who danced at the Roxy Theater, but when Radio City Music Hall opened in 1932, they were a big hit because of the way they looked on the stage—it's 144 feet wide—and they added twenty more dancers, and then four more, and they've been there ever since. They're all the same height, and they're all dressed alike—"

"I know what the Rockettes do," I said, but there was no stopping her. She was in full spate.

"They've done over a hundred thousand shows, and in the 1970s they *rescued* Radio City Music Hall! It was going to be torn down, and they went out in their Rockette costumes and stood all around the building, asking people to sign petitions to save the building. All eighty of them stood out there. In the middle of winter, when it was snowing and everything—"

I waited for her to pause for breath and then realized that wasn't going to happen. I was going to have to break in and stop her. "The Rockettes came out, and then what happened?" I asked.

"They formed this long, perfectly straight line. They were wearing these red leotards with white fur trim and hats and gold tap shoes. That's one of their traditional Christmas show costumes. They've been doing a Christmas show since 1933—"

At this rate, we could be here all night. I broke in again. "They formed a straight line, and then what?"

"They linked arms and kicked their legs in the air at the same time," she said, her eyes bright with excitement as she described it, "as high as their heads. And all the kicks were to exactly the same height."

I nodded. "That's what the Rockettes are known for. Their precision eye-high kicks."

"And then these skaters came out and skated on a pond—right on the stage—to the song 'A Simple Little Weekend'—"

From *Bumpy Night*.

"And then the Rockettes came out again in pale blue leotards with sequins on the top and silver tap shoes and kicked some more and then—"

Was I going to have to listen to a blow-by-blow of the entire show? "Emily," I said. "What exactly hap—?"

"And then they opened the curtain, and there was a toyshop, and the Rockettes came out dressed as toy soldiers, and they all fell down—"

The Rockettes were famous for that, too, the long line of ramrod-stiff soldiers collapsing like dominoes, one against the other, till they were all in a carefully lined-up pile on the stage.

"And *then*," Emily said, "they came out dressed all in silver with these square boxes on their heads and flashing lights—"

Robots, I thought. *Of course. In keeping with the theme of the Macy's parade and the department stores' Christmas windows.*

"And they all tap-danced," she said breathlessly, "and turned and kicked, all exactly alike. And that was when I realized...when you asked me the other night what I wanted to be, I didn't know what you meant. By wanting to be something, I mean. But now I do." She looked up at me with shining eyes. "I want to be a Rockette!"

My first thought was, *Thank God it's the Rockettes and not musical comedy!* I wouldn't have to compete with that youthful innocence, that disarming enthusiasm.

My second thought was, *How ironic!* Dr. Oakes had brought her here specifically to convince people artificials weren't after their jobs, and now here she was announcing she wanted one of the most sought-after jobs in New York. She was now a threat to thousands of aspiring Rockettes, and tens of thousands of little girls in dance classes all over America.

It's his own fault, I thought. *He should have known better than to have let her see them.* Even when they weren't dressed up like robots, they looked like them, with their identical costumes and long legs and smiling faces. And performed like them, their synchronized tap steps, their uniformly executed turns and time steps and kicks. Dr. Oakes should have known it was bound to dazzle her.

Add to that her youth (and I wasn't talking about her sixteen-year-old packaging, I was talking about her lack of experience—and who has less knowledge of the world than a robot?) and the fact that every little girl who'd ever gone to see them had come out of the show wanting to be a Rockette, and what had happened was inevitable.

And impossible. In the first place, she was designed to do photo ops and interviews with unsuspecting dupes, not dance. And in the second place, Dr. Oakes would never let her.

"You can't be a Rockette," I said. "You told me yourself artificials aren't allowed to take humans' jobs."

"But it's *not* a job!" she said passionately. "It's... jobs are tasks humans *have* to do to keep society functioning and to earn money to pay their living expenses. Being a Rockette is something totally different! It doesn't have anything to do with money. It's like a...a dream or a...a quest or...it's—"

"What I did for love."

"*Yes*," she said, and now I knew for certain she was stage-struck: she hadn't even noticed that was a line from a Broadway musical.

"But it's still a job," I said. "The Rockettes are paid—"

"They wouldn't have to pay *me*. I'd do it for nothing!"

"And even if artificials were allowed to take humans' jobs, there's still the problem of your height."

"My height?"

"Yes, you're too short. The Rockettes have a height restriction."

"I know. They're all the same height. What is it?"

"They're not actually all one height," I said. "That's an optical illusion. They put the tallest girls in the middle and then go downward to either end."

"Well, then, I could be one of the ends."

I shook my head. "No, you couldn't. You have to be between five foot-six and five-foot-ten, or at any rate that's what it was when I auditioned to be a Rockette. It may have gone up since th—"

"*You* were a Rockette?" she squealed, and it was clear I'd just gone up several notches in her estimation. "Why didn't...? It didn't say that in your bio."

"That's because I wasn't one. While the auditions were still going on, I got offered a part in the chorus of *The Drowsy Chaperone*, and I took it. It turned out to be my big break."

"But how could you give up being a *Rockette*? I wouldn't ever want to be anything else!"

It didn't seem like a good idea to tell her I hadn't actually wanted to be a Rockette, that I'd only auditioned because I'd hoped it might get me noticed, or to tell her that when I'd heard I'd made the chorus of *Chaperone*, I'd walked out of the Radio City rehearsal hall without a backward glance.

"You have to tell me what I need to do to become a Rockette," she said, clutching my arm. "I know you have to learn tap dancing—"

"And jazz dancing and ballet. *En pointe.*"

She nodded as if she'd expected that. "I can have those programs installed."

"A program of dance steps isn't the same as actually learning the steps," I said. "It takes *years* of training and hard work to become a dancer."

She nodded. "Like in *A Chorus Line.*"

"Yes, exactly," I said. "But even if you had that experience, it wouldn't matter. You're only— what? Five-foot-two, at the most?"

"One."

"And the height requirement's five-foot-six," I said, hoping the appeal to logic would convince her what she wanted wasn't a good idea, as had happened when she'd wanted to be named Eileen. "You're simply too short."

She nodded thoughtfully.

"I'm sorry. I know it's disappointing, but it's all part of being in the theater. I didn't get the part of Fantine in the revival of *Les Mis* because I was too tall. And Bernadette Peters lost the part of—"

She wasn't listening. "What about bingo-bongos?" she asked.

"What?"

"Bingo bongos. Should I have them done?" and when I still looked blank, "in *A Chorus Line*. The 'Dance 10, Looks 3' number. Val said she had the bingo-bongos done."

Indeed, she had. She'd been talking about having her breasts enlarged and her derriere lifted, or as she referred to it, having her "tits and ass" done, which I refused to explain to a dewy-eyed innocent. Or a robot.

"It wouldn't do any good," I told her. "As I said, you're not tall enough to meet the height requirement."

"What did you do in the audition?"

She was too stage-struck to hear a word I was saying. "I'm trying to explain, you won't make the first *cut* for the aud—"

"What did you have to do?"

"They taught us a series of combinations, which we did in groups of three. And then if we made callbacks, we had to learn a full routine, with time steps and kicks, and do a tap solo."

"What did you do for your solo?"

"'Anything Goes.' But you won't *get* to do a solo. You won't even make the initial cut. You're too short. And even if you met all the requirements, you'd only have a miniscule chance of getting in. Hundreds of dancers audition every year, and only one or two make it. I'm not trying to discourage you, Emily," I said, even though that was exactly what I was trying to do. "I'm just trying to be realistic."

She nodded and was silent for a moment. "Thank you for all the advice, Miss Havilland. You've been most awfully kind," she said and was out of the car and splashing down the street through the rain, which was coming down harder than ever.

"Emily!" I shouted, "Wait!" but by the time I got the window down, she was half a block away.

"Come back!" I called after her. "I know you're disappointed, but you can't walk home in this. Jorge will be back in a few minutes. He'll drive you home. It's late, and your hotel is *miles* from here."

She shook her head, flinging raindrops everywhere. "It's only forty-five blocks," she said cheerfully, and vanished around the corner.

Jorge, arriving moments later with two cardboard cups, was furious. "You let her walk home in the rain?" he said disapprovingly. "She'll catch pneumonia."

"She can't," I said, but he wasn't listening to me either.

"Poor kid," he muttered, pulling away from the curb with a jerk that spilled coffee all over me. "Poor little thing!"

"Poor little thing" was right. Because even if she could charm the choreographer into waiving the height requirement (which wasn't entirely out of the realm of possibility, given her programmed-in charm), there was no chance at all of Dr. Oakes's allowing her to be a Rockette. It would undermine the image he and AIS were trying to convince the public of. Even her raising the possibility of being a Rockette would be too dangerous. *He'll cut short their tour, and they'll be out of here on the next plane*, I thought. *If they haven't left already.*

But the next morning, there she was on TV, smiling and waving from the foot of the Statue of Liberty and later from a horse-drawn carriage in Central Park, and on Monday night there was coverage of her charming the pants off reporters and the TSA as she and Dr. Oakes went through security at LaGuardia on their way home, with no sign that she'd had her hopes dashed.

"Will you be coming back to the Big Apple soon, Emily?" one of the dozens of reporters asked her.

"No, I'm afraid not," she said, and there wasn't even a hint of regret in her voice. "I had a wonderful time here in New York! The Empire State Building and everything! I especially loved seeing *Only Human*."

Well, at least Torrance will be happy about her mentioning the play, I thought, waiting to hear what she'd say about the Rockettes.

"What did you think of the Radio City Christmas show?" the reporter asked.

She smiled winsomely. "I loved the nativity scene. They had real camels and everything!"

"Where do you go next, Emily?" another reporter asked. "Back to San Jose?"

"Yes, and then we'll be in Williamsburg for Christmas."

"And then L.A. for the Rose Bowl parade," Dr. Oakes said. "You're really looking forward to that, aren't you, Emily?"

"Oh, yes," she said, dimpling. "I *love* flowers! And football!"

"One last question," the reporter said. "What was your favorite part of your visit?"

Here it comes, I thought.

"Meeting Claire Havilland. She's *such* an amazing actress!"

I suppose I should have been grateful to her, especially when Torrance called the next day to tell me *Only Human* was sold out through Easter and three days later to say Austerman wanted to have lunch with me to talk about *Desk Set*.

But I wasn't. I was suspicious. That touching little scene in my car had obviously been just that— a scene, performed by a very skilled actress—and she hadn't fallen in love with the Rockettes at all.

But then what had its purpose been? To soften me up like Eve Harrington's made-up story about seeing Margo Channing in a play in San Francisco and falling in love with the theater, so that she could worm her way into my life?

I half-expected her to be in the audience on Tuesday night, in spite of the LaGuardia scene, but she wasn't, and on the way home after the show, Jorge told me there'd been a story on the radio about their arrival in California.

"Did she say anything about the Rockettes?" I asked him.

"No. She didn't say anything about your making her walk halfway across Manhattan in a rainstorm either." He glared at me in the rear view mirror. "You're lucky she didn't catch her death of cold."

She wasn't in the Saturday matinee audience either, or backstage after the show, and by the middle of December I had more important things to worry about, like Austerman's insistence on a dream-sequence number in *Desk Set* with me in, you guessed it, a leotard and fishnet stockings.

Add to that the management's decision to add an additional matinee to the schedule because of increased ticket demand, Austerman's wanting me to help audition the Spencer Tracy role, and every reporter in town wanting to do an interview on *Only Human*'s Tony nomination prospects. By mid-December I was exhausted.

Which was why I was taking a nap in my dressing room before the show when Benny the stage manager knocked and said there was someone to see me. "A Cassie Ferguson," he said. "She says she knows you."

"Cassie *what*?" I said blurrily, wondering if that was the name of Austerman's assistant. "What does she look like?"

"Blonde, tall, hot."

All of Austerman's assistants were tall, blonde, and hot. He was as bad as Miss Caswell's producer boyfriend. And if she was from Austerman, I couldn't afford to let her see me like this. The nap had added ten years to my face. "Tell her I'm doing an interview with *Tiger Beat* and I'll meet with her during intermission

He looked unhappy. "She said she needed to see you right away."

"Oh, all right," I said. "Give me five minutes and then send her in," and frantically started to repair my makeup, but almost immediately there was a second knock on the door.

Benny was right. She was a knockout: tall and leggy, with gorgeous long blonde hair, and, even though she was wearing a belted raincoat, it was obvious she had a great figure.

"Well?" she said. "What do you think?"

"Emily!" I said, staring. "My God! What—?"

"I had the bingo-bongoes done," she said happily.

"I can see that."

"I was just going to get longer legs, but the proportions didn't look right, so, since I had to get a new torso anyway, I thought I might as well get a new ass, like in the song, and new—"

"But why?" I said.

"To meet the height requirement," she said, as if it were self-evident.

Oh, my God, I thought. *She was serious. She's going to try to become a Rockette.*

"The upper limit's five-ten-and-a-half," she said, "but the median of the current Rockettes is five-nine, so I went with that and with thirty-six for my chest. I did a C so I could be sure I'd fit in a size six—that's the most common size costume. And people tend to be less intimidated by flatter-chested girls."

She untied the belt and opened her raincoat wide to reveal a spaghetti-strap black leotard and sheer tights.

"Hot" was an understatement. She had definitely had the bingo-bongoes done.

It was too bad Torrance wasn't here. "*This*," I would have told him, "is what one is supposed to look like in a leotard. Which is why I have no intention of wearing one in *Desk Set* or anywhere else."

"Do you think I should have gone with a D instead?" Emily asked.

"No," I said.

"What about my outfit? Is it all right for the audition? I analyzed audition videos and photos from the past ten years, and this was the most common, but some of the dancers wore colored leotards or leggings, and I was wondering if I should do that to make them notice me."

"Trust me, they'll notice you," I said.

"What about my shoes?" she said, sticking out her foot and pointing a toe in a T-strapped black tap shoe. "The audition brochure said character heels, but I didn't know if I should wear black or beige."

"Black," I said. "But auditions aren't till summer."

"I know, but they have a vacancy they need to fill."

Good God, I thought. *She's killed a Rockette*, and she must have guessed what I was thinking because she said, "A Rockette on one of the tours quit to get married, and they had to replace her with one of the New York troop, so they're holding a special audition."

"But you have to know how to tap dance—"

"I do," she said. "And I've learned jazz, modern, and ballet. Here, I brought an audition tape." She pulled out an android, swiped through several screens and handed it to me.

And there she was, tap-dancing, executing flawless time steps and cramp rolls and Maxie Fords—and the eye-high kicks the Rockettes were famous for.

"I've had all the choreography terms pro-grammed in, and I've memorized three different routines for my audition solo—'Anything Goes' and 'One' from *A Chorus Line* and 'Forty-Second Street.' Which one do you think I should do?"

"Emily—"

"I learned all the routines from the Christmas show, too, but I wasn't sure I should do one of those," she said. "Oh, and what about my hair? Is blonde okay? Sixty-two percent of the Rockettes are blondes."

"Blonde is more than okay," I said.

"And you think I look like a Rockette?"

Like the perfect Rockette. "Yes," I said.

"What about my face? The age requirement's eighteen, so I had it altered to look older—"

She had. Her cheekbones were more defined, and her face thinner, though it was still recognizably Emily's and had retained the wide, innocent eyes and the disarming smile.

"—But I was wondering if I should change it to look more like the other Rockettes. I made a composite of the current troop's faces, and it has a straighter nose and fuller lips."

And much less vulnerability, I thought. A-modern-woman-in-Manhattan-who's-had-lots-of-bad-experiences-and-worse-boyfriends face. The idea of Emily with that face was unthinkable.

And besides, if she was actually going to try and become a Rockette, she would need all the help she could get. And her face was her biggest weapon. *Well, not her biggest*, I thought. But definitely a weapon, as witness the reporters' behavior at that backstage interview. And Jorge's.

"What do you think?" Emily asked. "Should I change my face?"

"No," I said. "Absolutely not," and posed the question I should have asked in the first place, especially since he was liable to come bursting in here any minute. "What does Dr. Oakes say about all this? Did he authorize these changes?"

"No, of course not," she said. "He'd never let me do this. I got some of the engineers to help me."

"How did you talk them into it?" I was about to ask, and then realized I already knew. She'd charmed them just like she'd charmed Jorge and the TSA. "And Dr. Oakes didn't object?"

"No. He doesn't know about it. He's in Japan with Aiko."

Of course, I thought. *He's off introducing his artificials to other countries.* And different cultures would have different ideas of what was threatening about artificials. They'd require different models, all with faces and names carefully chosen to make them seem harmless: an Aiko even shorter than the original Emily for Japan and a Rashmika for India, a Mei-Li for China.

And meanwhile his American model had turned into a combination of Eliza Dolittle and Frankenstein's monster.

"I'm not sure you're right about my keeping the face," she said. "What if one of the Rockettes recognizes me? I met some of them that night at Radio City Music Hall."

And they'd have seen her on the news or in that interview with me. "So you were planning to audition as Cassie somebody?"

"Ferguson. Yes, because the rules say you have to be at least eighteen years old, and I'm only one."

One. But what a one! "Definitely a singular sensation," I murmured under my breath.

"You don't think I should do that?" she asked anxiously. "I know it's lying, but if they know I'm an artificial—"

They'll never let you audition, I thought. They'd have exactly the same reaction I'd had, and Emily was even more of a threat to them than she had been to me. As Torrance had said, actresses get where they are by being one of a kind, but with the Rockettes, sameness was the whole point.

And the Rockettes weren't stupid. They'd see instantly that if one of them could be replaced, all of them could, and that once the management realized they could have Rockettes who didn't want health benefits or time-and-a-half for overtime, it would be all over.

So she was going to have to lie and tell them she was a human. But she'd never get away with it. Even if she managed to fool them at the audition, she wouldn't make it through her first rehearsal. She didn't sweat, she didn't get out of breath, she didn't make mistakes. And she could learn an entire tap routine by watching it once. They'd spot her instantly.

Emily was watching me with a worried expression. "You don't think I should tell them I'm human?"

"I don't know. Let me think," I said, wishing I had Emily's computer brain to help me figure out what to tell her. I knew what I should tell her: the cold hard truth. That there was no way she could ever be a Rockette and she should go back home to San Jose and do what she'd been designed to do.

It would be much kinder than letting her batter herself to death trying, like a moth against a porch light. But I also knew she wouldn't listen, any more than I had when I was eighteen.

"What do you think?" Emily was asking me. "Should I put 'artificial' on my audition form?"

"No," I said. "You're not going to audition."

"But you can't become a Rockette if you don't audition."

"Only if you're an ordinary human," I said. "When does Dr. Oakes get back from Japan?"

"Not till the twenty-second. That's when we were supposed to go to Williamsburg for Christmas."

The twenty-second was a week away, but we didn't actually have that much time. AIS would already be looking for Emily. Multinational corporations don't just let a valuable piece of equipment walk away, especially one who was ruining any hope they had of selling the idea of artificials to the public.

On the other hand, they could hardly let it get out that one of their "perfectly harmless" robots had gone rogue. They'd have to look for her through private channels, which would slow them down. And even if they did decide to go public and had the police put out an APB on her, they'd be looking for a five-foot-one sixteen-year-old with light brown hair, which gave us a little time.

But the minute Emily went public, they'd come after her and Dr. Oakes would be on the first plane home from Japan. So we'd have to make sure that by the time he got here he wouldn't be able to do anything.

"All right, Emily," I said. "Here's what we're going to do. You're going to go on every news and talk and late-night show we can find and tell them how much you want to be a Rockette. You're going to tell them all those things you told me that night in the limo, how they started and what they've done over the years—dancing in the Macy's Parade and saving Radio City Music Hall. And you're going to tell them all the things *you've* done so that you could become a Rockette—how you learned to dance and memorized the routines and studied their history. We're going to convince them you deserve to be one of them."

That wasn't quite true. What we were going to do was convince the *public* she deserved to be a Rockette and hope the resulting pressure would force the Rockettes to let her in. "Do you remember the names of the talk show hosts who interviewed you when you were here for the Macy's Parade?" I asked her.

"Of course."

Of course. "Good. I want you to make a list of them and how we can contact them."

"Do you want me to call them and set up interviews?"

"No, we don't want anyone to know where you are till you show up for the interviews. I'm going to send you to my apartment—Jorge will take you—and I want you to use my computer to find some photographs of Rockette costumes. Preferably one of their Christmas costumes—if we can tie this in with Christmas, it will help. People love Christmas stories with happy endings. Find a photograph, and then call Jorge and have him come and get it and bring it back here to our wardrobe mistress—"

"Why?"

"So you can wear it to these interviews. We're going to arrange for you to dance as part of your appearances. You can do one of the routines you learned."

"But—"

"I know, it won't be the same as doing the routine with the Rockettes, but it's a way to show them what you can do. Think of it as your audition. You can do that, can't you?"

"Of course," she said. "It's just that a photo's not necessary. I've already made all the costumes."

"All the...you made all the costumes in the Christmas show?"

"No. I made all the costumes the Rockettes have ever worn."

The plan worked even better than I'd envisioned. Emily went on all the shows and tapped and talked her way into the audience's hearts, modeling an array of costumes from the costume of the original Roxyettes to Bob Mackie's "Shine," with its three thousand Swarovski crystals, to the merry-go-round horse costume the Rockettes had worn at the "last" performance, when it had looked like Radio City Music Hall would be torn down, and regaling her enraptured hosts with little-known facts about the Rockettes: that before coming to New York, they had danced in St. Louis as the Missouri Rockets; that in the days when they danced between movie showings, they had practically lived at Radio City Music Hall, sleeping on cots and eating at a special canteen set up for them; that in the open competition at the Paris Exposition, they had defeated the Russians and the *corps de ballet* of the Paris Opera.

"Lucille Bremer was a Rockette," she told them. "You know, Judy Garland's older sister

in *Meet Me In St. Louis*, and Vera Ellen, from *White Christmas*, but she kept showing off. A good Rockette never tries to stand out. She tries to dance just like every other Rockette."

And on every show and podcast she told the story of how the Rockettes had saved Radio City Music Hall, standing outside and asking passersby to sign a petition to make the building a National Landmark. "They went on TV and radio shows just like this one to plead their cause," she said, "and they all testified at the Landmark Commission Hearing. They did a kick-line with the mayor on the steps outside."

The audiences ate it—and her own eye-high kicks—up, and her appearances became instant Youtube hits. One, in which she talked reverently about why being a Rockette meant so much to her, went viral.

The only hitch was Torrance, who thought I was taking a huge risk by helping her. "It's dangerous," he said. "There's a lot of hostility to artificials out there. Some of it could spill over to you, and then there goes your Tony nomination."

"I thought you were the one who was convinced Emily was harmless," I said.

"That was before she decided she wanted to be a Rockette," he said disgustedly. "And why are you so set on helping her? I thought you hated her."

"I just didn't want her trying to steal my career. And if she gets to be a Rockette, she won't be, and Jeannette will be safe."

"Jeannette? Who's Jeannette?"

"The role I have been playing eight times a week for the past year," I said. "A fact which Emily would know."

"And that's why you're helping her? Because she knows what parts you've played?"

"Yes. And because if I get that Tony nomination you're so worried about me losing, it will be thanks to all the publicity Emily gave me. I'm just repaying the favor."

"Ha!" he said. "You know what I think? *I* think you orchestrated this whole PR thing to set her up."

Like Eve Harrington had set up Margo Channing, siphoning gas from her car and stranding her in Vermont so she could take her place.

"Are you sure you didn't put her on all those TV shows so Dr. Oakes would find out where she is and take her home?" Torrance asked.

And if I did, wouldn't that be a good thing? And not only for me, for everybody else who happens to be "only human?" I mean, she can rattle off the names of every play and musical and movie ever done and their cast lists *and* their song lyrics and librettos and dance routines and scripts. And when she was asking all those questions about what to wear to the audition, she'd said, "Should I wear my hair in a topknot?"

"No, a ponytail," I'd told her. "With a rose scarf to bring out the color in your cheeks."

"Should I make them pinker?" she asked, and she wasn't talking about makeup.

How can anyone compete against that? Or the fact that she'd never miss a step. Or forget her lines. Or get old.

Torrance was right. She *is* dangerous.

But I didn't say that. I said, "I'm just trying to help her. And me. If she's a Rockette, she can't steal Bunny out from under me."

"Bunny?" he said, looking confused. "Is that Margo Channing's husband? The one Eve tries to steal?"

"No. It's the lead in *Desk Set*. The musical Austerman's doing," I said wryly. "Ring a bell?"

If they turn her down for the Rockettes, I thought, *I'm firing Torrance and making her my manager.*

But it didn't look like they'd turn her down. After only two days of appearances, the public and press response to Emily was overwhelmingly positive, and the Rockettes who were questioned by reporters as to what they thought of her chances, said things like, "She knows more about the Rockettes than we Rockettes do," and "I don't know. I mean, I'm worried about artificials taking over and everything, but she wants it so *bad*!" and I thought, *Good God, she's actually going to pull it off.*

So it was a shock when she showed up after the Wednesday matinee. "I thought you were doing *The View*," I said.

She shook her head, looking so pale I thought her sensors must have malfunctioned. "They just changed the rules for being a Rockette so I don't qualify," she said.

"Then you'll have to do what you did before," I said firmly. "Change yourself so you do meet them."

"I can't," she said and showed me the new rule.

"No artificials," it read. *Only humans need apply*, I thought.

"Then we have to make them change the rule," I said.

"How?"

"We're going to make them look like monsters for picking on a sweet, harmless child like you. Do you remember the party scene from *Bumpy Night*? Where Margo Channing tries to expose Eve and says all those terrible things to her?"

She nodded.

"And do you remember how it backfired? How it made Margo look like a bully and Eve look like a victim? Well, that's what we're going to do. Can you cry?"

"No, but I can look really sad."

"Good. You're going to do that. And you're going to look helpless, and victimized. I want you to go watch *All About Eve* and memorize Eve's tone of voice and mannerisms while I write the script you're going to follow. You never wanted to hurt anyone or cause any trouble. You just admire the Rockettes so much!"

"But—" Emily said, looking up at me with those wide, innocent eyes. "I don't want to be Eve Harrington. She's not a nice person."

"Let me tell you a little secret, Emily," I said. "Nearly every actress is Eve Harrington at some point or other and has lied about her age or used her feminine wiles or taken unfair advantage to get a part. How do you think Margo Channing knew what Eve was up to?" I asked her. "Because when she looked at her, she recognized herself."

"Did you ever do anything like—?"

"Of course. I lied about my age and my Off-Broadway experience when I tried out for *Love, Etc.* And when I found out they'd moved the audition time I didn't tell anybody." And I had slept with the director.

"But I got what I wanted," I said. I looked at her. "How badly do you want to be a Rockette?"

And Dr. Oakes was wrong. He'd said his artificials had been designed to lack initiative, drive, preference. But once you wire in preference, even if it's only the ability to choose one word, one gesture over another, everything else comes with it. And when he'd put in safeguards against all those driving forces—lust and greed and ambition—he'd forgotten the most dangerous one of all, the one that overrides all the others.

Torrance wasn't the only one who could have benefited from watching a few musicals. If Dr.

Oakes had seen *A Chorus Line*, this never would have happened. And he'd have known what was going to happen when I asked Emily what she was willing to do to be a Rockette.

"Well?" I said, repeating the question. "How much do you want to be a Rockette?"

She raised her artificial chin and looked steadily at me. "More than anything else in the world."

She wanted to know how we planned to make the Rockettes management look like bullies.

"Do you remember how the Rockettes saved Radio City Music Hall?" I said. "Well, you're going to make them make you a Rockette the same way. What's the weather like this week?"

"A high of twenty degrees Fahrenheit with a rain-snow mix."

"Good," I said, remembering her standing outside my car in the rain, shivering and bedraggled. "I want you to wear the skimpiest Rockette costume there is, preferably something with a feathered headdress. And mascara that runs. And I know you don't wear mascara," I said before she could interrupt me. "But you're going to wear it for this. You're going to stand out there twenty-four hours a day looking half-frozen, asking people to sign a petition to make them change the rules so you can be a Rockette, and I'm going to see to it the media's there to film it."

I picked up the phone to call Torrance and have him arrange for the camera crews.

"But they know artificals can't feel cold or heat—"

"It doesn't matter, trust me," I said, thinking of Jorge, who still wasn't speaking to me. "I want you to shiver and do the teeth-chattering thing, and when passersby ask you if you're all right, you need to say, 'Yes, I'm just so *cold*!' and ask them to sign your petition."

"But won't the rain-snow mix run the signatures?"

"Yes, which is even better. It'll look like tears."

"But—"

"This isn't about getting signatures. It's about making the Rockettes management look like bullies."

"But I don't see how...Margo said mean things to Eve..."

"And they're making you stand outside," I said. "At Christmas. In the rain. Trust me, they'll look like bullies. And people don't like to look like bullies—or like the kind of people who'd let a historic landmark be torn down. They like to see themselves as the hero who rescues the building—or damsel—in distress. You stand out there in the rain in a skimpy strapless costume, and by Friday the Rockettes will be begging you to join them. And if it starts snowing, we'll have action by Thursday."

It didn't take even that long. When I called Torrance the next morning to ask him when the film crews were going to be there, he said. "There's no point in sending them. It's all over."

"You mean, they got rid of the 'no artificials' rule? That's wonderful!"

"No," he said. "I mean she's over wanting to be a Rockette."

"Over?"

"Oakes reprogrammed her."

"Reprogrammed her," I repeated dully. "When?"

"This morning. I thought you'd be pleased. It means you won't have to worry about her poaching your career anymore. Oh, and speaking of your career, Austerman called and said this'll be great publicity for *Desk Set*. You know, "'Only Human' Actress Sends Artificial Packing.' He said it'll make you a shoo-in for the Tony nomination. So it's just like the ending of *Bumpy Night*, only this time Margo wins the Tony, not Eve."

"It wasn't a Tony," I said. "It was the Sarah Siddons Award, which you'd know if you ever watched the play." *Like Emily did,* I thought.

"I don't know what you're so upset about," Torrance said. "She changed her height and her measurements and her hair color. This is no different."

Yes, it is. "Did they erase her entire memory?" I asked. "When they reprogrammed her?" All those plays and cast lists and lines, all that Rockette history.

"No, no, nothing like that," Torrance said. "According to Dr. Oakes, they just made a couple of adjustments to her software. They tamped down the preference thing so she wouldn't have such a strong response to the Rockette stimulus and adjusted her obstacle-to-action ratio. But she's still the same Emily."

No, she's not, I thought. *The real Emily wanted to be a Rockette.*

So here I am, standing in a freezing snow-rain mix in the leotard and fishnet stockings I swore I'd never be seen in, plus the trademark maroon-and-gold Rockette cap, which is doing nothing at all to keep the rain from dripping down the back of my neck.

I am clutching a clipboard for warmth and trying not to shiver convulsively as I accost passersby and attempt to get them to sign a petition to get Emily's software put back the way they found it and the Rockettes' rules changed so she can have a shot at her heart's desire.

And yes, I know artificials don't have hearts, and what about all the human girls out there between five-foot-six and five-ten-and-a-half with tap, jazz, and ballet experience whose job she'll be stealing?

And yes, I know I'm probably also opening the floodgates to a horde of robots whose dream it is to be ballerinas and neurophysicists and traffic controllers, and that I'll go back to my dressing room some night in the near future to find some disarming young woman who's the spitting image of Anne Baxter and wants to be my assistant, and I'll be really sorry I did this.

But I didn't have any choice. When I announced I wanted to be on Broadway, my mother told me I'd be mugged and raped and pushed onto the subway tracks, my father told me I'd end up broke and waiting tables, and the first three agents and five directors I auditioned for told me to "go back to Kansas and get married, sweetheart." Everybody had done everything they could think of to talk me out of it.

But they hadn't had me lobotomized. They hadn't cut out my stage-struck heart and replaced it with one that would have been willing to settle down in Topeka and have babies. Or adjusted my obstacle-to-action ratio so I'd give up and go home.

So here I stand, trying to blow some warmth into my frozen fingers and wishing I'd worn a warmer costume and that my skin turned rosy like Emily's when it gets cold.

It doesn't. When cellulite gets cold, it turns a mottled purple and ash-gray. The rain's washed away every bit of my age-defying makeup; I've completely lost my voice from calling to passersby to come sign my petition, so heaven knows how I'm going to get through tonight's performance; and Torrance dropped by a few minutes ago to tell me I was making a fool of myself and jeopardizing the *Desk Set* lead *and* the Tony.

And in three days out here I've collected signatures from exactly eighteen people, including Torrance (I told him if he didn't sign it, I was getting a new manager), Jorge (who said sternly, "Now you know how it feels to be made to stand out in the freezing cold,"), and a couple of teenagers who didn't care what they were signing so long as it got them on TV.

But the camera crews left an hour ago, driven inside by the icy rain and the fact that nothing was happening, and now it looks like it's going to snow, so the only thing that will bring them back is the discovery of my huddled, frozen body in a snowdrift. Even the tourists are giving up and going home. In a few minutes the only people left on the premises will be the Rockettes, and I haven't seen hide nor hair of them since I started this. They must be going in and out a door on the other side of the building to avoid me.

No, wait, here comes one out of the same side door Emily used that night she ran away to talk to me. The young woman's definitely a Rockette. Her coffee-colored legs are even longer than Emily's, and she's dressed like a Christmas present, with a wide candy cane-striped red and green sash slanting over one dark shoulder and tied in a Christmas bow at her hip.

She looks cautiously around, and I think, disappointed, *She's just sneaked out for a cigarette,* but no, after a second look around, she shuts the door silently behind her and hurries over to me, her character heels tap-tap-tapping on the sidewalk.

"Hi, my name's Leonda," she says, hugging her arms to her chest. "Brr, it's *cold* out here!"

"Did you come out to sign my petition?" I ask hopefully. The Rockettes resisted hiring minorities for a long time. They claimed audiences would be distracted if the Rockettes didn't all look exactly alike, including the color of their skin, and (according to Emily when she did the *Today* show) they'd resisted doing the right thing till 1982, when they'd finally hired the first African-American, and three years after that, the first Asian-American. Maybe Leonda heard Emily say that and decided she had to do the right thing, too, even if it *did* mean risking her job.

Or not. "Oh, no, I can't sign it," she says, glancing anxiously back at the side door. "I just wanted to tell you what a wonderful actress I think you are, Miss Havilland. I saw you in *The Drowsy Chaperone* when I was a little girl, and you were amazing!" She looks at me with starry eyes. "Seeing you was why I decided to be a dancer, and I was wondering if I could have your autogr—?"

"Leonda!" someone shouts from the door.

Another Rockette, dressed as a toy soldier, is leaning out, frowning. "What are you doing out here?" she says. "You've got to get changed! It's almost time!"

"I was just...sorry," she says to me and runs back to the door, her taps echoing on the wet pavement.

"I'll give you my autograph if you'll sign my petition," I call after her, but she's already gone back inside, and it's clear they aren't going to rise to the occasion like they did when Radio City Music Hall was about to be torn down. Or maybe Emily was wrong about them, and they weren't wonderful. Maybe they hadn't been trying to do something noble after all. They'd just been trying to hang onto their jobs.

And of course now that the two Rockettes are gone, a TMZ reporter and a cameraman with his videocam wrapped in plastic to protect it from the rain show up, looking annoyed. "Where are the Rockettes?" the reporter demands. "We were told to get over here because something was going on. So where are they?"

"There was one here just a minute ago," I say, but that's clearly not good enough, and to add insult to injury, a cab driver rolls down his window and leans out into the rain to shout, "Traitor! What the hell are ya doin' standin' out there trying to get a robot a job? Why don't you stick up for your own kind, lady?" and of course the cameraman's getting it all.

"That's First Lady of the Theater to you!" I shout back at the cabbie, and he waves a hand dismissively and drives off.

"How do you answer that question?" the reporter asks, sticking a microphone in my face. "Why *aren't* you sticking up for your own kind?"

"I am," I say. "I'm sticking up for the Rockettes and for the theater. They've always stood courageously for doing what's right," a speech which would have been more impressive if I thought it was true. And if my teeth weren't chattering. "I'm also, in spite of what you think, standing up for the human race. If we're going to make humanity such a hard show to get into, then we'd better make sure it's worth auditioning for by acting the way humans are supposed to."

"Which is?"

"Humane."

"And that's why you're doing this," he says skeptically.

"Yes," I tell him, but I'm lying. I'm not doing this to defend a noble cause, or because Emily looked like Peggy in *Forty-Second Street* or the poor, doomed heroine of *Our Town*.

I'm out here ruining my voice and my chance at ever getting a decent role again because that night in my limo, sitting there in her drenched coat, pouring out her nonexistent heart about tap steps and precision kicks, she had looked like me.

And I realize for the first time that that's why Margo Channing helped Eve Harrington. Not because Eve manipulated her into it, but because when she looked at her, she saw her younger, stage-struck self, that girl who'd fallen in love, who just wanted a shot at doing what she'd been born to do.

If they ever do a revival of *Bumpy Night* and I get to play Margo again, I'll have to remember that. It could add a whole new dimension to the character.

But at this point, getting the part—or any part, even Mama Morton—looks extremely doubtful. The reporter wasn't at all impressed with my "proud tradition of the theater and humanity" speech. For the entire length of it, he was looking past me, scanning for possible Rockettes.

But they're not going to show, and the reporter's apparently reached the same conclusion. "I told you they were getting us over here for nothing," he says to the cameraman.

The cameraman nods and lowers the plastic-covered camera from his shoulder.

"Let's go," the reporter says. "I'm freezing my balls off out here."

"Wait," I say, grabbing his arm. "Won't you at least sign my petition before you go?" But they're not listening. They're looking over at the side door, which is opening again.

It's only Leonda, I think—back for a second try at an autograph—which she is not going to get—but it's not. It's the Rockette who yelled at her before. She's changed out of her toy soldier getup into the Rockettes' signature red and white fur Christmas costume, and, as we watch, she pushes the door wide, braces it open with her gold-shod foot, and makes a beckoning motion to whoever's inside.

And out comes a Rockette dressed just like her who's...oh, my God! holding a petition. And on her heels is another Rockette. And another. And Leonda, who as she passes me turns her clipboard so I can see the petition and whispers, "I'd already signed mine. That's why I couldn't sign yours," and smiles a smile almost as sweet and disarming as Emily's.

"Are you getting this?" I ask the cameraman, but of course he is. Because what a glorious sight! They march out, heads up, chests out, as oblivious to the frigid wind as if they were Emily, even though I know it's cutting right through those tights, right through the toes of those gold tap shoes.

Here they come in a gorgeous, unending line that is going to go all the way around the building, every one of them in red leotards and white fur hats. And TMZ isn't the only one getting this. Other camera crews are arriving every minute, and so are tourists, holding up their cell phones and Androids to record this. Taxi drivers are slowing down to whistle and cheer, Jorge shows up with a cup of hot brandy-laced coffee for me, and even though the Rockettes aren't even all out the door yet, people are flocking around them, wanting to sign their petitions. And mine.

The only thing that could make this a better finale is if it would start snowing, which it does just as the last of the Rockettes step smartly out the doors. Starry white flakes fall on their white fur hats, their eyelashes, as they move into position, and their cheeks are almost as pink as Emily's.

They take up their places, eighty Rockettes— and, I find out later, thirty-two former Rockettes and every female dancer from *A Chorus Line*, *Forbidden Planet*, and *Almost Human*. And the chorus line from *La Cage aux Folles*. And they all stand there, backs straight, heads held high, facing into the bitter wind that seems always to be whipping around Radio City Music Hall, with their petitions and their fabulous legs and their knock-'em-dead smiles. And right now even I want to be a Rockette.

They're all in place now, every last one of them dressed in golden tap shoes and a red and white fur costume. Except for me. And the last eight out the door, who station themselves on either side of me, right beneath Radio City Music Hall's chrome-and-neon marquee.

They're dressed as robots.